epic!

VACATION

WRITTEN BY
GABE SORIA

ILLUSTRATED BY
RAFA RIBS
VINCENT BATIGNOLE

COLORS BY
WARREN WUCINICH

Andrews McMeel
PUBLISHING®

Bright Family created by Matthew Cody and Derick Brooks

Andrews McMeel Publishing
a division of Andrews McMeel Universal
1130 Walnut Street, Kansas City, Missouri 64106

www.andrewsmcmeel.com

Epic! Creations, Inc.
702 Marshall Street, Suite 280
Redwood City, California 94063

www.getepic.com

23 24 25 26 27 SDB 10 9 8 7 6 5 4 3 2 1

Paperback ISBN: 978-1-5248-7868-9
Hardback ISBN: 978-1-5248-7869-6

Library of Congress Control Number: 2022943706

Design by Dan Nordskog and Carolyn Bahar

Made by:
RR Donnelley (Guangdong) Printing Solutions Company Ltd.
Address and location of manufacturer:
No. 2, Minzhu Road, Daning, Humen Town,
Dongguan City, Guangdong Province, China 523930
1st Printing — 11/14/22

CHAPTER 1
A BRIGHT FAMILY VACATION

Boom?

Biiig boom.

Okay, I'll keep these little guys off your back. They're just sea babies in a confusing new world.

BONK

You sure you don't need my help?

Mom, I've got this!

Okay, okay! I wonder how your dad and brother are doing on the surface...

Jayden?

6

Whoa.

Whoa.

This kinda reminds me of the time we buried our goldfish Mr. Fins...

SHWIRL

Don't worry, honey. Those sea serpents are going to be fine.

It worked! They're back on their side of the closed portal!

Are you *sure*? Why don't I give you a *tour* before you decide?

You've already seen our *gold sand* beach, but did you know that we've terraformed our coastline so the waves are guaranteed to be *perfect*?

Plus, the water is always the *ideal* temperature!

And have you seen the *culinarium,* our gourmet restaurant? It's open 25 hours a day, 8 days a week!

Dulce de leche fountain!

Space ramen!

Roast beast!

Vegetarian roast beast!

Chef Vril Taxus-- he's famous!

There's also a mega *water park,* yo!

We've even got a *deluxe conference room* where scientists on vacation give lectures--when they're not getting relaxing massages, that is!

Vacation Scientific Lectures: The New Paradigm

11

14

15

That's why your dad and I made this plan for a little family reunion! After all, I haven't gotten to see much of you in the past few years.

"Do you remember that summer you came to visit me?"

"Best. Summer. Ever."

"That was *so* fun."

"I remember, Dad--they came back all dirty and scraped-up!"

You've got to *lighten up,* Benjamin.

These kids aren't going to *break* if you let them out of your sight.

Well, technically, we *could* break--

Grandpa's talking to your daddy.

I bet you've still got them studying those *Bright Family Safety Protocols,* huh?

What? Er, um...

Well, I had a long trip here, and I'm *hungry.*

Who wants Grandpa to buy dinner at that pizza place 'round the way?

Me!

Me!

Me!

Okay, Pop.

Grandpa, it's so much fun! You should try it.

Dad's **really** good at inventing stuff.

Oh, I'm okaaaaay...

You're **great** at it.

He even made our robot, Dusty!

Is that what you are? I thought Benjamin put some legs on the TV again.

Again?!

18

Your dad was a *wiz* on the melodica.

You never told us that!

You played in the band with Grandpa?

I'll tell you even more stories 'bout your dad while we spend the next few days taking a *culinary tour* of the city. Ramen for *everybody!*

Yay!

We've got a scheduling problem, Pop. Tomorrow morning we're going back to the resort planet.

Aw, mannnnnnnn...

Can't we just hang out with Grandpa for a few days?

Listen to your dad, kids. He's a busy man.

20

I want to hang out with Grandpa **and** party at the space water park.

Me too.

That's it! Of course! You kids are geniuses!

Grandpa could come **with** us!

I don't know-- Fleuben is only expecting us...

Don't be silly, Benjamin. There are enough free passes here for **all** of us.

Pleeeeease, Grandpa?

I bet they have some sort of campsite there. And you should **see** the buffet at this place.

They got ramen?

Space ramen!

I'll do it! Then I can say I've been to another planet--even if it is some cushy resort planet.

But what about this *portal* I suppose we'll be taking? What guarantee do I have that some bug won't fly in and crisscross my DNA?

Dad, please!

Is that a thing? Can it *do* that? Can I be a bug boy?

No, it's not a thing-- DNA safety protocols were the *first* safeguards I installed.

Sheesh! Do you think I'm some kind of--I don't know-- *mad scientist?*

It's 99 percent safe.

It's that 1 percent that worries me...

The next morning...

Okay, is everybody packed and ready to go?

All set!

This suit sure is **tight.**

You'll get used to it, Grandpa.

Where's your mom and Dusty?

They've gotta be around here somewhere...

Mom! Dusty! We're waiting for you.

Coming, honey!

Everybody ready?

Ready!

And do you *promise* that you'll try to forget about work while we're on vacation?

99 percent!

Let's go, already!

C'mon, Grandpa! It's weird, but it's *fun!*

It *can* be a bit disorienting, Pop, so please be careful...

Don't worry about me. As long as I've got my walking TV and don't turn into a bug, I'll be *fiiiiiiine...*

The explorer makes her way through the alien jungle, blissfully unaware that the foliage is teeming with life.

The noises of her new surroundings are strange--and alarming.

Huh?

CRACK

Just some native fauna, I guess.

But the explorer's bravery is stronger than her fear, and she continues on. And when she least expects it...

...the predator strikes!

Ahhh!

Gotcha, Nia!

Jayden! What are you doing?!

I'm acclimating to our new home.

We've only been here a few *hours.* Put your clothes back on and follow me. Mom and Dad want you back at the campsite.

Aww. I liked being free from the shackles of clothing and *civilization...*

Bright Family Vacation, Day 1.

Found him!

Great! Now the meeting can begin.

First, let's review the Bright Family Safety Protocols...

Groaannnn!

What? They're handy.

We **know** the protocols already, Dad.

And we **ignore** them all the time.

Okay, okay. Why don't you just give the situation report?

Yes! Thank goodness I brought my portable Smart Lecture Board.

As you can see, I've broken it down into three main elements, which I will break down even further...

Break it down, Dad!

Ahem. Yes. Thank you, Jayden.

Number one: The portal sent us to a mysterious *new* location, *not* the resort.

You hear that? We're not at the resort! That's science for you.

C'mon. I'm trying to be *methodical* about this.

Sorry, son. Carry on with the *science!*

Number two: We appear to be in an undeveloped jungle biome. So far, no hostile flora or fauna.

But there's still hope, right? *Right?!*

And three: The portal tech is offline, which means we cannot travel.

My conclusion: We should set up camp for tonight and tackle number three tomorrow. Questions?

34

Set up camp with what? We were supposed to be chilling in a fancy hotel!

I believe that I may be able to help with that...

...because I brought my *camping* backpack!

Dad, why did you bring your camping gear when we said we were going to a resort?

In case I didn't like my room.

I've got a tent! It'll be tight, but we'll make it work.

POP

I've got protein bars to keep us fed!

GRAM BAR

GRAM BAR

And I've got my trumpet for playing "Taps" at sunset. Because my philosophy is...

"Always think about what happens next!"

It's the Bright Scouts motto.

What are the **Bright Scouts?**

When your dad and his siblings were kids, I created our own family scout troop.

We had badges, a manual, camping trips--everything.

Including a motto.

I'm surprised you remember it.

It's only the basis of my entire scientific philosophy, Dad.

Oh. How about that?

36

And thinking about what happens next, I believe that we should--

Hold on a minute, son. I think what happens next is--

Um, who's the scientist with experience traveling to other worlds? Oh, that'd be me.

And who's the elder who knows best? This guy!

Well, *I* think what happens next is we explore a little bit more. Who's with me?

I'm with Mom.

I already covered the sectors of the jungle behind us. I say we go this way, toward the beach.

And you two, simmer down!

But he--

I was just--

Enough! We are stranded on an alien planet **together**, so you boys are going to have to learn how to get along.

Dad!

Mom!

Look!

Well, at least whoever lived here picked a planet with nice sunsets. Isn't this *great*?

Maybe we should just retire for the evening.

We could all use some rest.

Just a minute there, son. Turn around.

Oh, wow.

Allow me to play a little somethin'. A view like that deserves a send-off.

Jazzy version of "Taps."

That was really nice, Dad.

Reminded me of being back home.

Yeah, that was great, Grandpa.

Aw, it's nothin'...

Night!

Night.

Night.

Night!

Night, everybody.

Night.

Sweet dreams, TV with legs.

Bright Family Vacation, Day 2.

You're up **already,** Grandpa?

Up you wake, Bright Family!

I've got coffee for the adults and protein bars for everyone!

Except you, my friend.

Unless Benjamin invented a way for you to **eat.**

Thanks for the coffee, Dad. Nice design.

I know a thing or two about survival, Mr. Big Scientist.

I **was** the leader of the Bright Scouts, after all.

But there were only **three** of us!

You and your brother and sister were the little toes, and I was the **big toe** on that foot!

That's only four toes--

You know what I mean!

41

Okay, okay--enough talk about toes. Let's have a family conversation about what we're going to actually *do* about our current situation.

I'm glad you brought that up, Banira, because last night I took the opportunity to write a *new* chapter of the Bright Family Safety Protocols!

I can read it to you all, if you'd like.

Bright Family Safety Protocols: So You're Stranded on a Mysterious Planet

Grooooaaaaannn!

What?

That's like *homework!* On *vacation!*

Safety has its place, son, but I have a better idea.

Go on...

This place is **solid.**

With your help, we can make it a grade A shelter. Shouldn't take more than eight hours or so, I reckon...

Nope! That sounds like **actual** work! Just as bad as **homework!**

I have another idea: Why don't we just do...nothing? At least for now?

Nothing?

At all?

Think about it--we've got supplies and shelter.

The weather on this planet is wonderfully mild.

According to Dusty's sensors, it's 78 degrees, with 20 percent humidity.

The local fauna doesn't seem that interested in eating us.

Can I keep all of them?

And the geography looks pleasant!

I think we should spend some time at that beach.

It sounds a little...dangerous.

And slightly... frivolous.

Dangerous!

Dangerous!

Frivolous!

Frivolous!

Hey, where'd they go?

Look, a note.

Gone to the beach with the kids!

You two have fun together!

Love, B. ♡

Have fun? They left their wrist communicators behind!

That's *definitely* a violation of the safety protocols!

And this when we could be securing camp...

45

I'll be in my makeshift lab, working on the portal problem, Mr. Big Toe. Follow me, Dusty!

I'm going to do some shelter improvements. C'mon, TV!

GG

Dusty?

TV? Er, Dusty?

Woo-hoo!

Hahahaha!

Hey, kids! It's probably time to go back now.

Okay, Mom!

Mom, are Dad and Grandpa mad at each other?

What? No! They love each other--a lot.

But they're always kind of...arguing. Is it because they're so **different**?

Different? Ha! Those Bright men are **exactly** the same.

They just express their Bright-ness in their own way.

All they need is time to figure that out. Anyway, let's get back for dinner.

I wonder what your grandpa is cooking up. Probably not space ramen, I'm sorry to say.

Who needs space ramen when you've got all this tasty fruit? I'm actually okay with not making it to the resort.

About the resort... kids, I have a confession to make.

Hold on. Something's not right...

CRACK

CHOMP!

Shh!

There's something following us...

GULP

Y' evuh get th' feelin'...

48

TOK
TOK
TOK

I fixed up the exterior while you were in here portal gazing. So how's that going, Mr. Safety Protocols?

You should've been out there working with me! At least you would have gotten something *done.*

Slowly but surely, Dad. That's how you win the science race.

This is work, too! I'm only trying to fix the portal to get us *home.* Nothing *important* or anything...

I didn't say it wasn't important!

But you implied it!

I didn't mean it that way!

It sure sounded like you did!

Well, I'm sorry! Happy?

Yes! Thank you! Apology accepted!

Fine. Time to start working on dinner.

Where *are* Banira and the kids, anyway? They should have been back by now.

50

51

Haha! You should have seen the look on your face.

C'mon, Dad. Mind-reading machines don't exist.

Only because you haven't invented one yet! I know you...

It's getting dark. Let's get search partying...

Kids! Honey!

Hello?

Anything?

Nope.

Dad, I'm getting worried.

Son.

I know that you and I don't see eye to eye all the time, but I won't rest--*we* won't rest--until we find our family.

Yes, sir!

SNIFF SNIFF

It can't be!

Can't be what?

That aroma! It's...

It's...

It's **what?!**

I don't know about you, but I could swear I smell **space ramen.**

But Dad...

CHAPTER 3
THE LAST RESORT

That was pretty poetic, Benjamin. You should write that down.

Thanks, Dad.

But the galaxy's potential for beauty and wonder means it also has potential for *everything else*, too.

"Somewhere in this jungle, there might be *carnivorous alien plants* looking for their next meal.

"Or Jayden might have made friends with *cute aquatic creatures* and become the ruler of their undersea kingdom."

"That seems unlikely."

"Have you *met* your grandson?"

"Fair point."

"And then there are *extraterrestrial dinosaurs.* We can't rule *anything* out!"

But you're right--we have to trust that Banira and the kids know what they're doing.

And we also have to take care of ourselves while we search, so that means...

...time to *hydrate!*

GLUG GLUG

GLUG GLUG

I'm glad to see that you remembered your canteen.

Hey, once a Bright Scout, **always** a Bright Scout.

Speaking of hydration...

...this *Big Sipper* obviously indicates that an intelligent species is somewhere nearby--and that it likes iced tea.

Ooh, iced tea sounds *good.* This little fella wouldn't happen to have a soda fountain inside, would he?

Dad, I made Dusty to be a sophisticated autonomous robotic helper, not a drink dispenser.

Hey, it's a good idea for the *next* model.

No, Dad.

Okay--I think we've lost it. Let's get back to searching for Banira and the kids.

While we're at it, maybe I can figure out what's going on with this wrist communicator.

If I can get it to work, I can track their location!

TAP TAP

Or we could track them the Bright Scouts way...

Jayden's footprints!

And Banira's and Nia's--they must have come this way!

Dad... behind you...

It's nice that they have elevator music in space.

This song is ⸘huff!⸘ so familiar. It's...something Brazilian, right?

Good ear, boy. That's "Mas Que Nada," if I'm not mistaken.

Get ready, Dad.

PSHHT

I'm with you, son.

Ahhhhhhhh!

Jayden?!

Dad! Grandpa! Dusty!

Where's your mom? And Nia? Are they okay?

Okay? Are you kidding?

71

"...that began when the kids and I were walking through the jungle."

Yes, it's *me*, Bright Family...

...Fleuben, your favorite intergalactic resort manager!

But what are you doing *here*, on this uncharted planet?

Uncharted? Are you kidding? This is *my* planet!

Your planet?! But where are the luxury accommodations?

Where's the space ramen, man?

Didn't your mom let you in on her plan?

Her plan?

Say *what*?

I can explain.

73

So...when your grandpa and dad started butting heads back on Earth, I thought it'd be a great idea to get them talking.

Like, *really* talking.

"I made a call to Fleuben and told him my idea. Luckily, he had something *perfect* in mind.

"And right before we made our portal jump, I had Dusty change our coordinates to the ones Fleuben gave me.

"We also 'fixed' the portal so we couldn't just go back when your dad figured out we hadn't hit our target."

"Mom, that's so...crafty! Nice one!"

"I learned from the best, Jayden."

But...where are we *now*?

You're *almost* exactly where you intended to be--the portal simply took you to the other side of the resort.

The *other* side?!

75

78

And that's when the Bright Family's vacation really began. There was feasting!

Relaxing!

And family time!

But all vacations must come to an end.

Thanks again, Fleuben. We'd love to stay, but the kids have school tomorrow.

There'll always be a warm bowl of space ramen waiting for you at this resort, Bright Family!

With extra...

...spiiiiiiiiice?

Woo-hoo! Home again, home again, jiggly pig!

I don't think that's how that goes.

Who cares?!

Sooooo... anybody up for some late-night jazz? There's a jam session at a club downtown.

Not me! I'm gonna find out if antigravity beds can actually work here on Earth.

And I'm beat from all that relaxing.

WEEKLY JAZZ JAM

DOWNTOWN

I'm going to read the latest issue of *Science Hero Weekly*. You boys have fun together.

What are you looking for, Dad?

I've been carrying this in my pack for *years.* Figure it's time to finally give it to you. After all...

...you've earned it.

Aw, Dad...

Thank you.

I have your progress reports for the semester, students. Here you go, Mr. Bright.

I know you can do better.

Hmph.

RIIIING!!!!

RIIIIINNG!!

Remember, class: These need to be signed by *Monday!*

87

Hmm. This is...

...almost as bad as mine!

It's not funny! This has *never* happened to me before.

Well, there's a first time for everything. You should see *my* report.

Pee-*yew!*

Ha. I can smell it from here.

Right?!

A little while later...

So let me get this straight-- **both** of you bombed?

Bombed is a bit of an overstatement, Mom.

Ka-**boom!**

But what **happened?** I mean, Jayden I can see. But **you**, Nia...

Hey!

I'm sorry--that was unfair. But your father and I expect **much** more from you kids.

These progress reports are way below your abilities. There have to be **consequences.**

So as of right now, all your weekend activities are **canceled.**

94

But I was supposed to go to Natalie and Caroline's birthday party!

And I was gonna read *comics* all weekend!

Nope, and nope. Instead, you two are coming with *me* this weekend.

To your boring *conference?!* Nooooo!

Mom! Please! Be reasonable!

This *is* me being reasonable. This weekend, you two are going to be my interns. Maybe a bit of *work* will straighten you out.

Work?! Aw, Mom!

Are we at least going to take a portal to the conference?

No way. Portal travel is making you kids soft. We're doing this the old-fashioned way...

No complaining on my jet. Think some deep thoughts! Enjoy the ride!

Why didn't *Dad* have to come and work, too?

Because he's got important research to do.

Research?! He's just playing with his terraforming program.

Yeah--he's playing *games!* Why does he get to play games?!

Hold on--I'm getting a distress signal from a whale rescue ship. And it's nearby!

Dusty, circle the jet and be ready to pick me up!

WHOOSH!

Anyway, Dad didn't have to come because *Dad* isn't the one who brought home such disappointing grades.

Suzuki-Bright Superconcentrated Fire-Extinguishing Grenade

I know you can do better! You're Brights!

FIZZLE!

But school is kind of *boring*, Mom.

Boring, Nia?! Since when?

It's not portal-hopping, that's for sure.

Portal travel and school are *entirely* different things, Jayden.

Let's talk more about this later. We're approaching our destination.

Where are we going, anyway?

Didn't I tell you? Only one of the neatest places in the world...

Nice landing!

Thanks, Nia.

What happened to *Osaka* Osaka?

It's still right next door. They just built this one because there was a big demand for it. They needed *more* Osaka, so...voilà!

Did they consider calling it...*Mo'Saka?*

I can't wait to explore. The geoengineering of artificial islands is *super* interesting.

While you do that, I'm going to try *all* the okonomiyaki* stands.

*Japanese cabbage pancakes--a popular street food now and in the future!

Remember, kids-- this is a *work* trip.

Awww.

Wow! Look at this place! Does it have a swimming pool?

Probably, but you two are going to be too busy to swim.

I'll have your bags taken to your rooms. Enjoy the *boring science conference*, Dr. Suzuki-Bright.

I will! I'm sure it's going to be *very* dull.

???

What's going on, Mom? What kind of conference is this, anyway?

Shh! Not here. The *boring conference* is just an elaborate cover story.

This way, kids. Then I'll tell you what's *actually* going on.

"I got the idea while we were at Fleuben's resort. There we were, Earthlings, peacefully interacting with a vast variety of interstellar beings.

"I had a vision of a future where the people of the galaxy shared ideas, knowledge, and culture!

"But it had to start somewhere.

"It took months of intergalactic conference calls and logistics emails, but all that effort finally paid off!"

Fleuben, can you mute your microphone? I'm getting a lot of echo.

Oops! Sorry.

We organized the inaugural Transdimensional and Intergalactic Science and Goodwill Summit!

We're having it in Neosaka because I want the delegates to see what Earth can bring to the cosmic table, but we don't want to reveal that aliens exist...yet. Hence all the secrecy.

Awesome, Mom! And sneaky.

Mom, this is **amazing!**

So what do you need us to do? Mediate a scientific discussion? Deliver a lecture on our experiences?

Are we audiovisual support?

No, but your job is still **incredibly** important...

"You'll be handing out souvenir tote bags and helping out however you're asked."

Welcome to the first Transdimensional and Intergalactic Science and Goodwill Summit.

Have fun having fun. Enjoy your tote bag.

I can't believe it. We're in the coolest town on Earth, and we're stuck at the swag table.

The most important scientific conference in the galaxy is happening meters away, and we're handing out tote bags.

Tote bags!

There isn't even any free local *candy* in here. Being an intern is the *worst.*

Here come some people.

One tote bag, coming up.

Here's your complimentary tote bag, ma'am. You can, uh, carry your son in it?

Um...

And look at this cute little fella! What's your name, little guy?

I am Prime Minister Anfonio Braxas, intern! And this is my daughter, Fielgorf!

But...she's so...*big.* And you're so...*little.* How...

Ahem! That's how the life cycle of our species works--our children begin life as titanic, clumsy babies, then slowly but steadily shrink into compact and nimble adults like me. Interns should know these things!

A reverse life cycle... fascinating.

The galaxy is *wild*...

Look at the time! I'm late for a lecture. Interns!

I assume your duties include entertaining the children of conference delegates? Very well.

I'll see you later, Fielgorf!

Mom *did* say to help out however we're asked.

She sure did!

Hi, Fielgorf. I'm Nia Bright, and this is my brother, Jayden. We're from Earth!

Nice to meet you both!

So...I say we ditch the tote bag stand. Who's with me?

Me!

Me!

Cover for us, Dusty! C'mon, Fielgorf.

Can we explore the city? I've read all about Neosakan okonomiyaki, and I really want to try some.

You're speaking my language, Fielgorf. You ever been to Fleuben's resort? Their space ramen is...

~SMOOCH!~

It's Mom! Hide!

What's happening here? I'm confused.

Our worlds have been rivals for hundreds of cycles!

The Braxsonians know what they did.

The Pelosians started it!

My father says--

Nope!

This conference is supposed to be about pandimensional and galactic *understanding*--not old rivalries between our *parents.*

You get me?

We get you, Nia Bright.

When you put it like that... *truce!*

Great! Now let's check out Neosaka... *together!*

Okonomiyaki!

Later, back at the conference...

Excellent keynote speech, Dr. Suzuki-Bright! This conference is going to be *great!*

CLAP

CLAP

I hope so. There's a lot that could go wrong with these different cultures interacting, but also *so much* that could go *right.*

Er--speaking of *so much that could go wrong...*

I left Fielgorf here, with those two interns! It's a Pelosian plot-- a plot, I say!

And Gilbort was last seen in the company of *your* child! So *you're* the plotter!

Whoa--what's going *on* here?

Well, the Braxsonians have been at odds with the Pelosians for *forever,* and vice versa. It's a classic *planet versus moon* rivalry.

If my Fielgorf isn't found immediately, this means war!

I was going to say that! You copied me--again!

Sigh...

KAIJUBILEE

...I think I found a solution.

Moments later.

Gotta hand it to you, Jayden. This is cool.

Isn't it?!

Rawr!

I love it!

We blend right in!

And bonus: We. Look. *Great.*

117

Meanwhile...

...Braxonian treachery!

...Pelosian skulduggery!

Excuse me, but is everything okay in there?

Everything is fine! It's just a, uh, private viewing of a sports contest!

The Braxsonians versus the Pelosians... doing sports! Against each other!

What's happening in there, robot?

Dusty! Whatever you do...

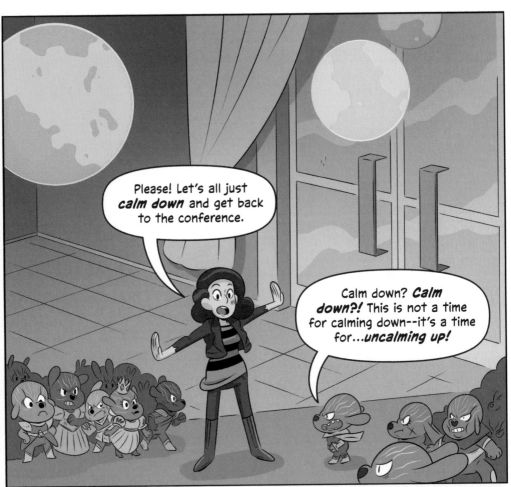

Please! Let's all just **calm down** and get back to the conference.

Calm down? **Calm down?!** This is not a time for calming down--it's a time for...**uncalming up!**

Uncalming up?

Exactly.

This isn't the time for methodical analysis! You and your children are part of this plot against us!

Yes! Exactly!

Why would we do that? I organized this conference to be a beacon of unity, and my children are committed to the cause as well!

No, they're in league with *you* and plotting against *us!*

They're in league with *you,* and plotting against *us!*

Lunch has arrived, Dr. Suzuki-Bright. Maybe a meal will calm them down?

Good thinking. We'll discuss intergalactic conflict resolution over lunch.

Maybe some food will make them less cranky.

Pelosians... to arms!

Onward, Braxsonians!

This is *not* happening. A *food fight* is *not* breaking out at my conference to promote intergalactic understanding and peaceful cooperation.

I'd say it's more of a *culinary skirmish.*

Not helpful!

I'm calling Nia and Jayden. If they're with Fielgorf and Gilbort, they need to get back here before this *culinary skirmish* becomes an all-out **FOOD WAR**.

Does this mean I should push the "Time Travel: Multiple Alternate Futures" seminar back?

It's time travel, so I guess *when* it happens isn't so important...

RING RING

Mom's calling.

You think she realized we're not handing out tote bags?

Uh, hi, Mom. What's up?

Nia! Thank goodness. Where *are* you?!

Well, Jayden and I met these two cool alien kids, and we thought we should show them around--

Well, those *cool alien kids* are the children of Prime Minister Braxas and Empress Nacreeb. You need to get them back to the hotel *now!* Or else...

"...it's *war!*"

We're on our way! Let's go, everybody!

I'll be back!

127

Shouldn't we **do** something?

You're right. We should. That's why I called the kids.

The kids?!

If we interfere, we'll fix a symptom and stop a food **fight.**

With the kids' help, maybe we can cure the disease and prevent a food **war.**

Dusty! Any sign of them?

Hi, Mom! We brought you some okonomiyaki.

Thank you, Jayden, but I'm *really* not hungry. What are you kids *wearing?!*

Actually, never mind.

I'm sorry we were gone for so long, Mom. We were just having such a good time hanging out with Gilbort and Fielgorf.

You made a mistake.

But maybe that kind of *hangout* is exactly what our current situation needs.

Gilbort and Fielgorf, I presume?

Yes, ma'am.

Your parents are worried sick about you, and because of the grudge between Braxsonians and Pelosians, a war is breaking out.

I need you to show them that peace is possible!

We'll work together!

And lead by example!

Aaahhh! Giant monsters of legend!

Flee!

Braxas, this is a threat neither of us can defeat alone.

Are you proposing what I believe you're proposing?

Yes...

...the first-ever Braxsonian-Pelosian *alliance!*

Together, we shall overcome. To arms!

131

This is... not going well.

What are you talking about? This is **awesome!**

We have to do something. Jayden, follow me.

Hey! Please! Hold on for just a moment.

There's more of them!

Renew the assault-- with salt!

They won't listen!

They don't recognize you. Take off your hoods!

Oh!

Why didn't we think of that?

Hold your fire! It's us-- Fielgorf and Gilbort!

A Pelosian and a Braxsonian...**together?**

What is this absurdity?!

They're working together, just like **you**, Prime Minister Braxas and Empress Nacreeb.

At first, they weren't happy about hanging out together.

But they learned that it's a lot easier to get along than it is to hold a grudge.

We're sorry about leaving the conference. Jayden and I didn't mean to start a diplomatic incident. We just wanted to explore a new place with new friends.

It's too bad kids from different galaxies don't get to come together like this more often.

Indeed.

Absolutely.

I'm just glad you're back, Gilbort.

Likewise, Fielgorf.

Glad that's settled. But who's going to clean up this mess?

I elect my diplomat daughter and her little brother because before they fixed everything, they helped break it.

I guess that's fair.

Aw!

The next day...

What a successful conference, Dr. Suzuki-Bright! Speaking on behalf of all Braxsonians, we look forward to the next one.

And thank *you*, Nia and Jayden. You brought our children together and showed us the folly of our old ways!

All credit goes to the kaiju costumes.

Jayden!

It was so cool hanging out with you two.

Totally!

Thanks to you, we're going to be pen pals!

Bye, everybody!

All right, kids. Locked in a course for home and letting the autopilot take over.

After we put on our space suits, anybody up for an in-flight movie?

Kids?

Is everything okay?

Yeah...no...I don't know.

Is this about your progress report? I think I overreacted. I'm sorry for making you feel bad about that.

Thanks, Mom.

I guess I'm just...a little sad. This weekend was *so* cool. Meeting those kids, helping broker peace between old rivals...and now what?

It's just that...after all the *stuff* we've seen across the galaxy, school back on Earth just seems...

...kinda *boring!*

Yep! That's it.

I still *like* school, and I love to learn, but I can't stop thinking about how much *more* is out there.

C'mere, you two!

SQUEEZE!

Oof!

Dusty, please take care of the landing. Kids, I have an idea, and I need to call your dad.

Later that evening...

What do you think they're working on down there?

I don't know, but Mom was really excited about it.

Nia! Jayden! Come down to the lab. We have something to show you!

What's going on?

You'll see. Ready, Benjamin?

Just putting on the finishing touches. Okay... done!

You two gave me a lot to think about this weekend, and I realized that your father's current terraforming work might be a solution to our problem. Benjamin?

You see, my project isn't a *game*--it's a *reality.* I've been using nanotech, portals, and robots to experiment with terraforming an out-of-the-way planetoid.

But your mom had a brilliant idea for a practical application of the tech, so we cooked up a little proof of concept to show you.

So you're terraforming a *planetoid?* Cool! But what does that have to do with us?

Please say kaiju planet, please say kaiju planet...

You two have *everything* to do with it. You *inspired* it.

Show them, Benjamin.

ABOUT THE AUTHOR

GABE SORIA is the creator of the Midnight Arcade series (Penguin Workshop) and the cocreator of the comic book *MegaGhost*. His other works include DC Comics' *Batman '66*, *Fakespeare in the Park*, a tie-in novel for Cartoon Network's *Regular Show* (Penguin Workshop), and the best-selling Audible Original *Foreverywhere*, created with Steve Burns of *Blue's Clues* and Steven Drozd of the band The Flaming Lips. He lives in New Orleans, where he's currently writing an original fantasy adventure trilogy for Penguin Workshop.

ABOUT THE ILLUSTRATORS

RAFA RIBS is a Brazilian artist currently living in São Paulo. He has worked as a character designer and visual development artist for animation and games for the last six years. He loves drawing imaginary universes and filling them with otherworldly characters and stories. Besides drawing, he likes playing indie games and going to music festivals.

VINCENT BATIGNOLE started his professional journey working on Serena Valentino and Ted Naifeh's comic series GloomCookie. Now living in Paris, he illustrates and writes for various international clients while earning a master's degree in cinema history and film analysis. When he's not drawing, you can find him playing video games, watching scary movies, or rummaging through book stores to grow his gigantic collection of manga drawn by CLAMP.

ABOUT THE COLORIST

WARREN WUCINICH is a comic book creator and part-time carny who has been lucky enough to work on such cool projects as *Invader ZIM*, *Courtney Crumrin*, and *Cat Ninja*. He is also the cocreator of the YA graphic novel *Kriss: The Gift of Wrath*. He currently resides in Boston, Massachusetts, where he spends his time making comics, rewatching '80s television shows, and eating all the tacos.

WRITTEN BY
GABE SORIA
ILLUSTRATED BY
SEAN DOVE
COLORS BY
SAM BENNETT

151

I think we're getting closer to earlier today... yes, there I am!

Let's see if I can get my attention...

Tachyon *nudge!*

ZZZZZ!

Whoa! What was *that?*

Huh. It almost felt like time-traveling tachyons... anyway, good night!

Rats! My plan's not working. All I can do is give myself tachyon *goosebumps.*

Get the cake, Benjamin! Get the cake!

Well, if you can't *remake* the past, maybe you should concentrate on *making* the future.

What do you mean?

Our memories are wonderful, but what if you just focused on making *new* ones with the kids?

You're absolutely correct. Heading back...to the present!

It's too bad this invention didn't work the way you wanted.

It's probably for the best. Messing with the time stream can get, well, *messy*.

Where's the cake?! Is it back here?

Jayden, I hate to admit it, but--

You forgot my cake, didn't you?

I did, and I'm sorry. I'll do my best not to forget again. But for now, let's have some fun!

LOOK FOR THESE BOOKS FROM

FREDERICK COUNTY PUBLIC LIBRARIES

AVAILABLE **NOW!**

TO READ MORE, VISIT
getepic.com